Forgottenville™
The Town That Arrested
SANTA CLAUS™

Story by:

FRANK McQUILKIN

Novelization by:

PAUL T. MALINOWSKI

Illustrated by:

FRANK ROCCO
CLAYTON STANG

Art Director:

DOROS EVANGELIDES

TSM Productions, Inc.
40 Whitney Avenue
Syosset, N.Y. 11791

THIS BOOK IS
THE
PROPERTY
OF

Tasla Dilevo

Enjoy!

AND IS
A
GIFT
FROM

Cousens Sak.
Boys
12/25/93

Far, far away, in a land of perpetual ice and snow, snuggled under a protective hill, stands the magic workshop and home of Santa and Mrs. Claus.

In the kitchen, Mrs. Claus is busily preparing dinner for Santa. She knows he will be hungry when he comes home from making toys for girls and boys all day.

"My, oh my," says Mrs. Claus. "I think this pie is just about done. Yes, indeed! And doesn't it smell good! I'll have a fine supper for Santa tonight."

And as the cuckoo starts to toll the hour of 6:00 p.m., Mrs. Claus says:

"Oh, my goodness! That means Santa will be here in no time!"

Meanwhile in Santa's workshop, the head elf sings:

"It's time, it's time,
It's time, it's time,
It's time to stop making toys;
It's time to stop working for girls and boys.
It's time, it's time,
It's time, it's time,
It's time to stop carving wood;
The cuckoo clock tells us we should
    stop making toys,
    stop making noise,
    stop all our work
    for girls and boys.
    Put the dolls to sleep.
    Stop the soldiers' feet.
  Give our hands a rest.
  Everyone knows we've done our best."

"Well, Santa," says the head elf, "the cuckoo said it's 6:00 p.m. and I guess that means it's time to stop making toys for today."

"Oh, ho, ho and so you are right," says Santa. "Put the dolls to sleep, stop the soldiers' feet, give your hands a rest, I see you've done your best. That was a fine day's work. Now let's go home and have a good supper."

"Goodnight, Santa," say the elves. "We'll see you tomorrow." And they all hurry home for the night. And so does Santa because he can hardly wait for his supper.

After he has had his supper, Santa sits down in his easy chair to watch TV and have some of the pie that Mrs. Claus has made for him. He says:

"That, Mrs. Claus, was a splendid supper, and this pie is delicious, too."

"I'm so glad you enjoyed it, Santa," says Mrs. Claus, "and how did work go today?"

"Oh, ho, ho...fine! Just fine! We are right on schedule," says Santa. "Boys and girls everywhere should get pretty much what they want for Christmas this year. Of course, there's always..." Suddenly, Santa notices something on TV and he says, "Wait a minute, Mrs. Claus. Something is happening on TV."

"...We interrupt this program for a special bulletin," says the newscaster. "The rumor mentioned on our regular newscast earlier this evening has just been confirmed. A town has actually been discovered. It has been hidden by deep forests and high mountains for nobody knows how many years. The town, quite appropriately, is called Forgottenville. We shall continue to bring you details as we receive them. Now, back to the Happy Hour."

And as the newscaster finishes his story, Santa turns to Mrs. Claus and says, "A completely forgotten town. You know, Mrs. Claus, I'll bet the town of Forgottenville has never heard of me."

"My, oh my," worries Mrs. Claus. "And Christmas is only a short time away. You must tell them quickly. After all, what is Christmas without Santa Claus?"

Indeed, what would Christmas be like without Santa? And so, as Santa and Mrs. Claus prepare to go to Forgottenville, there is one person there who will not be happy about their arrival. He is Dr. S. Neak, Mayor, and owner of every business in Forgottenville. He has just heard the news on his secret shortwave radio.

"Arrgh!" cries Dr. S. Neak. "First, that mountain-climbing reporter and now this! Santa Claus is coming to Forgottenville. *This is my town!*" he shouts. "Just like my ancestors, I own it and everything in it! I even own the people! But if Santa Claus comes, everything will change. I can't have that! I won't have that!"

He leaps from his chair and paces up and down while he thinks. Suddenly he stops.

"Wait a minute," he sneers. "I've always given the people any modern invention I thought was good for them. Let them think I'm bringing them Santa Claus...and when he's here!...Heh, heh, heh..."

So the town of Forgottenville, hidden all these years in mountains and forests, finally learns about Santa Claus. On the day of Santa's arrival a parade is held on Main Street. Santa and Mrs. Claus ride in his sleigh, pulled by his faithful reindeer, while behind them march jugglers, clowns and even a brass band. In the crowd of townspeople that has gathered along the street, is Billy. He is sitting atop his big brother Tom's shoulders. Billy's mother and his little sister Nan are also there. Everyone is enjoying the parade very much. As the cavalcade continues down the street, Tom tells Billy, who is blind, what is happening.

"That's the band passing right now, Billy," says Tom. "They're all marching in step, all making music together."

"What are they wearing?" asks Billy. "Do they have uniforms?"

"Oh, yes!" replies Tom. "Their uniforms are bright blue and...oh...do you remember what blue looks like, Billy?"

"Of course I remember what blue looks like, Tom," laughs Billy. "How could I ever forget blue?"

"Oh, Billy! Here come Santa and Mrs. Claus," says Mother. "They are on a big, beautiful float and they are waving to everybody. They're waving to us! Look, Nan, over there. Wave, Nan wave!"

And as Santa waves to the crowd, he says to Mrs. Claus, "Well, Mrs. Claus, this is quite a welcome, isn't it!"

"Oh, yes, Santa!" agrees Mrs. Claus. "My, oh my, they are certainly glad to see you."

"This afternoon I have to ask all the boys and girls what they want for Christmas," says Santa.

"Be sure you keep an accurate list Santa, so you don't forget anyone," warns Mrs. Claus.

"My dear!" replies a shocked Santa Claus. "I would never forget anyone at Christmas."

Later, as the children line up and wait to tell Santa Claus what they want for Christmas, Mrs. Neak prepares to finish the candy she is making.

"Is the candy ready yet?" shouts Dr. S. Neak as he storms into the kitchen.

"It only needs another minute of stirring," answers Mrs. Neak shyly. "Then I can pour it out and it will cool in no time."

"Here, let me stir while you get the pans," says Dr. S. Neak, still shouting.

And as Mrs. Neak hurries off into the next room to fetch the pans, Dr. S. Neak slips a small bottle out of his pocket. "Heh, heh," he says, reading the label on the bottle, "Elixir of Selfishness." Then he empties the contents into the kettle of candy mix as he continues to stir. He puts the bottle back in his pocket before Mrs. Neak returns with the large candy pans. And as they lift one of the kettles from the stove to pour the candy into the pans, Mrs. Neak asks, in a quiet and shaky voice: "Whatever made you think of giving the children candy? I mean ... uh ... it's such a *n-n-nice* idea."

"It just came to me when I was talking to Santa Claus," replies Dr. S. Neak, chuckling deviously to himself.

And so, as Santa sits listening carefully to what each child wants for Christmas, the other children wait anxiously in line for their turn to sit on Santa's knee. It is a long line, stretching almost to the door of S. Neak's Dry Goods and Notions Store. Dr. Neak walks along the line, offering candy to those who are waiting. Although he tries to smile affably, he succeeds only in sneering a little more than usual.

"Have some candy, little girl?" asks Dr. S. Neak. But she hesitates, shyly half-hiding behind her mother's skirt. "Oh, do! It is very good. Mrs. Neak made it."

"Only one, Agatha," warns her mother. As the little girl starts to eat the candy, Dr. S. Neak moves on, offering candy to the others in line.

Santa continues to ask the children that come to him, "What do you want for Christmas? And what do you want for Christmas?", over and over again.

But, something strange has happened to the children of Forgottenville as they think about that question. They are more than restless. Some of them are punching each other and hitting their parents who are trying to stop them. The children's faces have changed, expressing greed, anger, frustration and even hatred. The boys and girls of Forgottenville have become infected with greed and selfishness.

The children start to riot, snatching things from counters, trying to take them from each other. There is much pushing, kicking and screaming. The children are completely beyond control:

I want! I want! I want! I want!
This and that
And something more,
A dog, and a cat,
And everything
Or...
I'll cry,
I'll stomp,
I'll shout,
I'll shake;
I'll do anything to get my cake.

I want! I want! I want! I want!
I want some toys,
I want some games.
I'll have the same.
And more, of the more!

I want! I want! I want! I want!
This and that
And something more,
A bike, and a kite,
And everything
Or...
I'll cry,
I'll stomp,
I'll shout,
I'll rage;
I'll do anything to get my way!

Dr. S. Neak opens the door and motions to someone outside. Two guards come in. After talking to Dr. Neak, they make their way through the rioting children to Santa Claus.

"I'm afraid we'll have to ask you to come with us, Santa Claus," commands the first guard.

"Come with you?" cries Santa. "Where...where do you want me to go?"

"We're arresting you, Santa Claus," replies the other guard, "for disturbing the peace of Forgottenville."

Santa cannot believe his ears. "Arresting me?" he says, "Santa Claus? Santa Claus in jail?"

And so it is, Santa Claus is arrested and put in jail.

The next morning, Mrs. Claus is finally allowed to see Santa. He is sitting on his cot in his cell, looking very sad and dejected, but he jumps to his feet when he sees Mrs. Claus coming.

"Oh, Santa!" cries Mrs. Claus, running to him. "This is the most terrible thing. Oh my! I'll bet you didn't get a wink of sleep last night."

"Now, now, my dear," says Santa, hugging her. "Calm yourself. I'm as well as can be expected. Come, sit down here."

As they sit, Mrs. Claus frowns as she feels how hard the cot in Santa's cell is.

"Now tell me what's happening," Santa says, soothingly.

"Well, your trial will be this morning and...oh...oh-oh..." and Mrs. Claus starts to cry.

"There, there, it can't be all that bad," comforts Santa.

"Oh, Santa, it doesn't look good," Mrs. Claus continues, dabbing at her eyes with a handkerchief. Your lawyer says they're accusing you of making every child in town selfish and greedy, and...and...he says he can't find any witnesses to come to your defense."

"No one...to defend Santa Claus?" asks Santa in disbelief.

"Can't you think of some *boy,* or *girl,* who didn't become selfish?" worries Mrs. Claus.

"There has to be at least one, there just has to," ponders Santa. "Let me think...hmmm...Wait! Yes! There was one! Now I remember."

"Oh, Santa, tell me!" says Mrs. Claus.

"It's all clear now, my dear. He was one of the first. He came and sat on my knee...a fine young fellow he was...and suddenly I realized he was blind."

"Oh, Santa!" cries Mrs. Claus.

"I asked him what his name was," continues Santa, "and he said...'Billy, Santa Claus. My name is Billy.'"

"'That's a fine name, Billy,' I said. 'And now, what do you want for Christmas?'"

"And he said, 'I want a pair of brown boots, size nine, and I want a yellow dress, size six...'"

"'One minute, Billy,' I asked. "What do you want these things for?'"

"He smiled at me and said, 'Well, the boots are for my brother, Tom; the dress is for my sister, Nan; and my mother needs a new coat. They're right here, watching.' And so they were."

" 'Well, what about *you*? What do *you* want for Christmas?' " I asked again."

" 'That's what I want, Santa Claus,' Billy said. 'Boots for Tom, a dress for Nan, and a coat for Mother. And I'll be very happy to have those things. Thank you very much.' And as he started to walk to his family he stopped, looked toward me and said, 'Oh, Santa Claus! Did I tell you what color dress?' I said, 'Yes, Billy. Yellow, wasn't it?' "

" 'That's right!' he said. 'Thanks again... and have a Merry Christmas!' 'And...a Merry Christmas...to you, Billy,' I said."

"No one could say Billy was selfish," Santa continues. "If only that boy could be found, Mrs. Claus, I'll bet he'd come to my defense."

Suddenly, the guard appears at the cell. "You'll have to go now, Ma'am," he says. "The trial will be beginning soon." Mrs. Claus kisses Santa and tells him, "I'll find him for you."

"Oh, if only you could!" shouts Santa as the guard leads Mrs. Claus out of the cell. "It's all up to you now, my dear. It's all up to you."

And so Mrs. Claus, wearing a very determined look, emerges from the jail. She bounds into Santa's awaiting sleigh and picks up the reins.

"Up and away we go!" she commands and the reindeer-drawn sleigh dashes down the street and disappears in the distance.

Meanwhile, unaware of Santa's distress, Billy and his family are decorating their small home, with what meager Christmas decorations they could muster.

"Do you think I would look pretty in a yellow dress, Mother?" says Nan, gleefully.

"I think you look lovely in any color, Nan," replies Mother. "Now do help me with these decorations."

"Hello, everybody! Look what I've got!" calls Tom, as he comes in from outside, stomping the snow from his feet.

"Oh, Tom," says Mother. "How lovely. Billy! Come feel this holly. But watch out you don't scratch yourself." Billy gathers the holly carefully in one big armful. His mother bends to pick up a few scattered leaves and sees Tom's very wet and worn boots. "Oh, Tom," she says sadly, "Your feet are so wet! How badly you need a new pair of boots."

"I don't need them any more than you need a new coat, Mother," he replies.

"That's the kind of thing you're supposed to want for Christmas," adds Nan, "and Santa will bring it to you. I know what I want."

"Well...I know what I want," declares Tom.

"And I, too," whispers Mother. "What about you, Billy?" she continues. "What do you want Santa Claus to bring?"

"Yes, Billy, what Christmas gift do you want for yourself?" asks Tom.

"A Christmas gift for me?" proclaims Billy. "I'd want my gift to be...

A Christmas gift for me?
I want my gift to be
A pretty ring for you,
A gold one, brand new.
You'll walk along the street,
Show it to all you meet.
That's what my gift will be;
That's what I want for me.
A Christmas gift for me?
I want my gift to be
A new silk dress for Nan,
A yellow one, if Santa can;
A woolen coat for my mother
And leather boots for my brother.
That's what my gift will be;
That's what I want for me.
A Christmas gift for me?
I want my gift to be
Gifts for all of you."

And as Tom and Nan applaud, Mother gives Billy a warm hug and kiss. Suddenly there is a commotion outside. Someone is frantically pounding on their front door. Mother rushes to the door and quickly opens it. Before her stands Mrs. Claus.

"Why, Mrs. Claus!" exclaims Mother. "What a surprise! What...what can we do for you?"

"Santa Claus needs Billy's help," replies Mrs. Claus pleadingly.

"Me? Me? cries Billy. "I'd do anything to help Santa Claus!"

And so, as Mrs. Claus tries to bring some help for Santa's defense, Dr. S. Neak, the prosecutor, prepares his case against Santa. Mrs. Neak finds herself with a day to herself, at home, away from the overbearing Dr. Neak.

"Well," she says, "he'll be busy for the rest of the afternoon at any rate. Now to enjoy myself a little."

She goes to the kitchen cupboard and takes a book and a dish with two pieces of candy.

"He didn't even suggest that I keep some of the candy for myself," she moans, "but I did."

And so Mrs. Neak sits down in one of the chairs in the living room. She puts the candy on the table beside her, and still muttering to herself, begins to read her book.

While she reads, her cat, which had been sleeping in front of the fireplace, suddenly pops open one eye and starts to sniff. Stealthily, he gets to his feet. Slinking toward the table, the cat jumps into a chair and stretches a paw across the table for the candy dish. At the same time, Mrs. Neak, engrossed in her book, reaches for the candy. She touches the cat's paw just as he snatches one piece of the candy and pops it into his mouth.

"Oh!" cries Mrs. Neak, jumping with fright. "I hope you're satisfied, scaring me half to death. And you've taken a piece of my candy!"

She takes a swipe at the cat with her book. "Scat! Go back to the fireplace, you good-for-nothing," she scolds. The cat bounds from the chair and scampers back to the fireplace where he sits watching Mrs. Neak, stroking the rug with his tail. Mrs. Neak takes the other piece of candy and bites off a very small chunk. "Umm! I must say that is good, even if I did make it," says Mrs. Neak as she looks at the cat. "Oh, don't sit there trying to make me feel ashamed," she continues. "I didn't mean it." Mrs. Neak gets out of the chair and crosses to the cat to pet him. "It's all right. I didn't mean it," she says.

The cat's hair bristles and he starts to make a snarling sound that is almost a growl. As Mrs. Neak reaches to pet him, the cat spits and swipes at her hand with his claw. A very startled and shocked Mrs. Neak jumps back from her suddenly crazed cat. The cat tears around the room, up the long window drapes and jumps to the top of the cupboard, where he crouches, snarling and spitting like a cornered tiger. Something is happening to Mrs. Neak, too. Her placid expression is changing to...a picture of viciousness. Her eyes blaze and her mouth twists into a sneer that could easily match her husband's.

"So you want to play!" snarls Mrs. Neak at the cat. "Well, I'll fix you!"

And she whirls and snatches up the hearth broom and strides toward the cat. As Mrs. Neak makes a swipe at the top of the cupboard, the cat jumps over her to the table. Mrs. Neak whirls and swats at the table, just missing the cat who bounds to the floor. She chases the cat around the room, trying to swat him with the broom. Frightened, the cat rushes out an open door. When Mrs. Neak reaches the door, she stops, sways as though faint and clutches the door frame. Her neat hair is now partially undone and hanging in wisps. Her dress is somewhat disheveled and she is breathing very heavily. She turns and totters toward the chair and sidetable. When she reaches the table, she leans on it as she catches her breath.

"What has come over that cat?" she gasps. "For that matter, what's come over me?" She gasps again and then her eyes light on the candy dish and the piece of candy with a tiny bite taken from one corner.

"The candy! It was the candy," she says. "And I *didn't* dream that I saw Dr. Neak putting something in it. But what am I going to do?"

Mrs. Neak stands irresolute for a second, then snatches up the piece of candy and puts it in her pocket. "Blaming Santa Claus for the trouble," she cries. "Well, we can't have that!"

And Mrs. Neak storms out of her house and hurries along the sidewalk. She wears a big cape that sags off one shoulder so that part of it trails in the snow. She also carries an umbrella which she swings as she walks, sending snow flying with every blow, while she loudly sings:

"I want! I want! I want! I want!
    This and that;
    I'll cook his goose.
    A man like that
    Should not be loose.
    And...
    I'll speak
    My piece;
    I'll singe
    His fleece!
    Around his neck I'll put a noose!"

Meanwhile, Santa Claus' trial is set to begin. It is a typical courtroom scene: the jury in its box, Santa Claus at a table beside his lawyer, the prosecutor summarizing his argument for the jury, while the judge listens attentively. The prosecutor is, naturally, Dr. S. Neak. The courtroom is packed with spectators.

"...And so, you have heard the evidence, ladies and gentlemen of the jury," says the prosecutor. "You, yourselves, have seen how this once-peaceful town of Forgottenville has been changed by this visit from Santa Claus. Where once we had happy, contented children, we now have children seriously infected with *greed* and *selfishness.* All they're interested in now is what they are going to get for Christmas. And all that was caused by the man sitting in front of you." He finishes, pointing at Santa Claus, who looks most uncomfortable.

There is an ugly murmur from the spectators and the lawyer turns to whisper to Santa Claus.

"I'm afraid it doesn't look good, Santa," he says.

"Order in the court! Order in the court!" shouts the judge as he pounds his gavel.

As the prosecutor continues, the members of the jury seem to be tending to agree with what he says.

"You have heard my worthy opponent warn us that if Santa Claus is convicted and put in jail, millions of children all over the world will suffer," he says. "They will not receive any Christmas gifts. But, let me ask you this question, ladies and gentlemen of the jury: if those children have become as greedy and selfish as the children in Forgottenville, do they deserve those gifts? Should we reward selfishness and greed? NO! NO!" he continues. "And the very fact that the accused cannot produce one witness in his defense is conclusive proof, ladies and gentlemen, that you should bring back the only verdict possible for Santa Claus: *GUILTY!*"

"Not guilty!" shouts Billy from the back of the courtroom. "Santa Claus is not guilty!"

Billy and Mrs. Claus have arrived and are making their way down the aisle. The spectators turn to see what is going on.

"Mrs. Claus," cries Santa, "you've found him! That's the witness I need!" Santa says to his lawyer.

And as Billy reaches the judge's bench, he looks up and says "I'll tell you the whole story, Your Honor, and why Santa Claus is innocent."

And so after Billy has told his story, the jury leaves to make their decision as to whether Santa Claus is guilty or innocent. After some time, the jury files back to their places; they have finished their deliberations. When they are seated, the judge speaks:

"Ladies and gentlemen of the jury," he says, "have you reached a verdict?"

"We have, Your Honor," says the foreman as he stands.

"Will the defendant please rise and face the court," says the judge.

Santa Claus rises, looking anxiously to where Mrs. Claus and Billy are seated. He then takes two steps forward facing the judge.

"What is your verdict?" continues the judge to the foreman.

"Guilty as charged, Your Honor," states the foreman. The verdict is received with mixed emotions by the people in the court. Some applaud, some boo.

"Order in the court! Order in the court!" shouts the judge once again, pounding with his gavel.

The foreman continues. "...but, in view of the defense witness's testimony, the jury feels there are extenuating circumstances and would like to make a recommendation."

"And what is your recommendation?" asks the judge.

"We recommend that Santa Claus be granted probation on this condition: that from now on he ask children two questions; first, what do you want for Christmas? And second, *what do you want to give for Christmas.*"

"Santa Claus? ..." says the judge.

But again there is a commotion at the back of the courtroom and Mrs. Neak's voice is heard.

"Wait! Wait! You've got the wrong man!" she shouts. Mrs. Neak rushes into the space before the judge's bench where she confronts her husband.

"There is the man who caused all the trouble," announces Mrs. Neak, as she points to Dr. S. Neak. *"My* husband; *your* butcher and baker, your prosecutor, your Mayor. He put something in the candy he gave the children that made them act the way they did. I can prove it."

Dr. S. Neak, the prosecutor, glares at her but at the same time cringes before the stern look of the judge.

"This is most perplexing," exclaims the judge. "I've never had a case like this before. Should I arrest Dr. S. Neak and discharge Santa Claus?"

"NO! NO!" says Santa. "Christmas is a time of understanding. Let us think that Dr. S. Neak did what *he* thought was best for Forgottenville, and realize that he did all of us a big favor, especially me. If the children had not turned greedy and selfish, I would never have learned what a mistake I have been making all these years. From now on, I shall ask two questions and put the emphasis on "What do you want to *give* for Christmas?"

"Then," says a very relieved judge, "the court rules, based on this new evidence presented by Mrs. Neak, Santa Claus is cleared of all charges. This court is adjourned. Oh, and...Merry Christmas everyone."

And so Santa Claus is surrounded by Mrs. Claus, Billy and many cheering spectators. Dr. S. Neak tries to slip away through a side door. However, Mrs. Neak sees what he is doing and rushes to him, driving him out, prodding him along with her umbrella.

That night, Billy's family decorates their Christmas tree. Santa and Mrs. Claus are there, seated by the fireplace. Billy, on Santa's knee, joins in the merriment.

"If it were not for you, Billy," says Santa, "I wouldn't be sitting here so comfortably tonight. I'd be...in jail!"

"My, oh my!" cries Mrs. Claus. "What would the children of the world have done for Christmas gifts if Santa had not been able to visit them? Wouldn't that have been terrible?"

"Yes," agrees Santa, "...but I've got to remember to ask them two questions from now on: what do you want for Christmas? ..."

"What do you want to *give* for Christmas?" chimes in Billy.

"Right!" says Santa, "...still one thing puzzles me. Why weren't any of you children affected by the candy?"

"You've forgotten," explains Tom. "We wanted meeting you to be something special for Billy, so Nan and I weren't in the line. We weren't offered any."

"And since I really couldn't take four pieces — one for Mother one for Nan, one for Tom and one for me —" finishes Billy, "I said, 'No, thank you' and didn't take any."

"I see," says Santa.

"Santa, I'd like to ask you something," Billy says.

"What's that, Billy?" asks Santa.

"Well...you're always asking people what they want for Christmas, but what about you? What do you want for Christmas?"

"Billy, the answer to that is something I've learned from you," says Santa. "A Christmas gift for me? I'd like my gift to be...

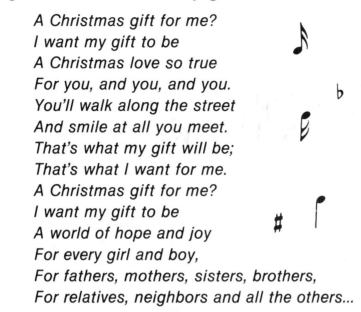

A Christmas gift for me?
I want my gift to be
A Christmas love so true
For you, and you, and you.
You'll walk along the street
And smile at all you meet.
That's what my gift will be;
That's what I want for me.
A Christmas gift for me?
I want my gift to be
A world of hope and joy
For every girl and boy,
For fathers, mothers, sisters, brothers,
For relatives, neighbors and all the others...

My friends...that's what my gift will be; that's what I want for me. A Christmas gift for me? I want my gift to be gifts for all of you!"

WILL I CUCKOO

Narrative and Original Music and Lyrics
available in stereo album and cassette.

PRINTED IN U.S.A.   GRAPHICS BY EAST COAST GRAPHICS, INC. • N.Y.